Bella the Buttercup Beach Fairy

KAY MURRAY

Balboa Press books may be ordered through booksellers or by contacting:

Balboa Press
A Division of Hay House
1663 Liberty Drive
Bloomington, IN 47403
www.balboapress.com
1 (877) 407-4847

Because of the dynamic nature of the Internet, any web addresses or links contained in this book may have changed since publication and may no longer be valid. The views expressed in this work are solely those of the author and do not necessarily reflect the views of the publisher, and the publisher hereby disclaims any responsibility for them.

This is a work of fiction. All of the characters, names, incidents, organizations, and dialogue in this novel are either the products of the author's imagination or are used fictitiously.

Any people depicted in stock imagery provided by Getty Images are models, and such images are being used for illustrative purposes only.
Certain stock imagery © Getty Images.

ISBN: 978-1-9822-2854-5 (sc)
ISBN: 978-1-9822-2855-2 (e)

Library of Congress Control Number: 2019906575

Print information available on the last page.

Balboa Press rev. date: 08/30/2019

BALBOA
PRESS
A DIVISION OF HAY HOUSE

Just a sparkle beyond the human mind lies a magical

World for all to find.

Turn the page and

Step inside.

If we quiet our minds and go deep within, in a Sparkle of light you can see Bella take flight. Making her very fairy magical home in the sand dunes on the edge of the deep blue sea. Where waves of mystical blues and sea foam green splash to the shore for all the world to see. With her wings spread wide she flits among the buttercups and sprigs of sea oats popping up high. Caressed by the sunshine swaying to and froe as the wild ocean breezes blow. Dressed in sparkles of sea salt shimmer in her buttercup bikini delight she loves her beach life with all her might.

It is early May and such a glorious day! Spring has sprung and there is so very much left to be done. Bella is working so very hard everyday cleaning and clearing away all sorts of trash and old fishing lines left behind. As drops of buttercup pixie dust drip from her body as pure as her very soul. She is creating a magical sparkling safe yellow flower power pixie pathway that all will come to know.

As Bella relaxed under the full moon glow she could feel the winds of change and a stir of energy from deep below. As the waves rushed to the shore Bella's eyes widening searching more and more. As the moon rises higher and higher sparkling across the deep blue sea she saw a large creature emerging. With a surge of excitement OH MY! I wonder who this could be, exclaimed Bella.

It is one of her oldest and dearest friends Sassy Susie the sea turtle has returned to lay her eggs once again. As Sassy Susie pulled herself high upon the beach, Bella greeted her with a big grin. It is so wonderful to see you again, said Bella. With a loving reply, it is so very wonderful to see you my dear. I look forward to our visit each and every year, said Sassy Susie. I have cleared a magical sparkling safe yellow flower power pixie pathway for all to see safe and free from debris, expressed Bella.

As Sassy Susie dug a huge hole, she and Bella chatted heart to heart and soul to soul. Preparing to Lay her eggs placing herself comfortably above, she dropped them gently in one by one. Pushing the sand back over her eggs keeping them safe and warm, deep in the earth free from harm.

After a short rest it was time for Sassy Susie to return to the sea and reunite with her own magical world Beneath. Please, oh please stay safe and free, expressed Bella. Until we meet again my sweet little Buttercup fairy friend on this very beach where we both began.

Bella took her job very seriously making sure all the many nest were safe from predators, humans and Even big storms. She watched over them day and night making sure everything was just right. until it was time to hatch and meet all of her new friends with tiny shells on their backs. As the full moon rises once again shedding her brilliant light, illuminating a pathway to the sea for the baby sea turtles to be free. The slope of the beach, the white caps of the waves and natural light of the ocean horizon helps lead their way.

Bella flitted from nest to nest as each baby turtle emerged. they followed the luminous glow leading them to their ancient ocean home. Following the magical sparkling safe yellow flower power pixie pathway. they are all coming to know. As the waves lovingly lapped their tiny shells triggering a knowing deep within. They are to return to this very beach again and again and again. Laying their eggs here just as their mothers. grandmothers and great grandmother sea turtles did.

After Bella's last fair well wishes, blowing loving energy kisses rippling through the breeze settling deep into the sea. Supporting her newly arrived friends, that she will most certainly see again and again. Watching over their baby sea turtles, just as she did them.

In one quick flit Bella was gone. Lighting on the brim of a little yellow buttercup rim. She smiled and giggled and wiggled in sheer delight. as the last baby sea turtles swam out of sight. She curled herself up in a little yellow buttercup bidding them all a wild and wonderful ocean life.

Printed in the United States
By Bookmasters